SUKIRAN SCHOOL

# THE VICKSBURG VETERAN

*A Southern slave mart, where blacks were bought and sold at auction*

# THE VICKSBURG VETERAN

## By F. N. Monjo

### Illustrated by Douglas Gorsline

SIMON AND SCHUSTER

NEW YORK

*Dedicated to the memory of my grandfather,*
WALTER WEV BAHIN,
*who first told me about the Vicksburg campaign*

# Contents

*Fred Grant and his father*

*Buck,*
*Julia, and*
*Nellie Grant*

# 1. Running the Guns

*April 16, 1863*

We were all waiting on the top deck
of the steamer *Magnolia.*
She was tied up on the river bank
at Milliken's Bend.

"It's nearly ten o'clock," said Pa,
looking at his watch.

"Nearly time," said Ma.
My little brother, Jesse,
was asleep in her lap.
My sister Nellie was sitting
next to Pa.
My other brother, Buck, and I
were standing at the rail.

Mr. Dana and a lot of army officers
were with us, too.
The night was dark and quiet.
There was no moon.
Way down around the bend in the
river, we saw the lights of Vicksburg.
The town was high up on hills that ran down to the
Mississippi River.
One by one, the lights went out.
The steamship rocked gently.
The river gurgled
in the night, and slapped at the hull.

"When will the Rebs start shooting,
Fred?" said Buck.

"As soon as they see our ships,"
I said.

"That's right, Buck," said Pa.
"Our ships have to run past
fourteen miles of cannon.
The Rebs have fourteen miles of cannon
up on top of those hills."

"We will make it, Ulyss," said Ma.

*On board the* Magnolia

Pa just smiled at Ma.

"General, I agree with Mrs. Grant,"
said Mr. Dana. "I believe our ships
will make it, too."

"Cump Sherman says it can't be done,"
said Pa.

"Cump Sherman isn't half the general
you are, Pa," I said.

Everybody laughed except Pa.

"Now, Fred Grant," said Pa, "I want you
to refer to General Sherman as
General Sherman. That's an order, you rascal."

I said, "Yes, sir."
My Pa is General Ulysses S. Grant.
When he gives an order, you obey it!
I think Pa's the best general
in the whole Union Army.
He and his friend General Sherman
have been trying to capture
Vicksburg for nearly six months.
We have tried four times,

*Gen. William Tecumseh ("Cump") Sherman*

but the Rebs have beaten us four times.
So now we are trying again.
Only, this time, Pa's trying
something risky.
He's sending ships down the river
tonight, right past the Rebels.
They're going right past the guns
of Vicksburg.
I hope they get past safe.
If they do, then Pa can march his

soldiers down below Vicksburg.
He can march them to a place
where there aren't any cannon.
Then the ships can take Pa's
soldiers across the Mississippi.
And if the soldiers can cross
the river, maybe Pa
can capture Vicksburg.

"There they go," said Pa.
Eleven dark ships began

*The quiet waterfront at Vicksburg, Mississippi*

chugging down the river.
For ten minutes, everything
was black and silent.
Then the Rebs in Vicksburg
saw the ships in the river.

*Boom* roared the cannon on the hills.
*Boom! Vroom! Ba-room!*
"Looks like the whole town
is on fire," said Buck.
But it was only the cannon.

*Union ships running the gauntlet at Vicksburg*

Our ships sped up, trying to run
past the guns.

*Boom! Vroom!* roared the cannon.
The sky was bright as day.
A half hour went by, then another.
The cannon never stopped firing.
One of our ships was hit.
She blew up.

"Oh, Ulyss! Look there!" said Ma.

"Don't you worry, Julia," said Pa.

The wreck of the ship caught fire.
It drifted down the river.

*Boom! Vroom!* roared the cannon.
The other ships kept chugging along.

"They're halfway past," said Pa.

"I count three hundred and ten
cannon shot so far," said Mr. Dana.

"I hope they don't wake Jesse," said Ma.

"You think they'll make it, Pa?" said Nellie.

Pa didn't answer. He just kept
staring down the river.

18

*Mr. Charles A. Dana, of the War Department*

Half an hour later, the cannon
fire slowed down.
Then the firing stopped.
   "It's midnight," said Pa.
   "Five hundred and twenty-five
shots by my count," said Mr. Dana.
   "We made it, Julia!" said Pa.
"We made it, boys!"
He slapped his knee.
"Ten of our ships got through!"

## 2. Hard Times

*April 28, 1863*

I've started keeping a diary
of everything that happens.
Guess what happened first!
Pa said I could come along with him
and the army, and be a soldier!
Ma said all right, since I'm
nearly thirteen. She says I can
go back to school after it's all over.

Then Ma took Buck and Nellie and Jesse
back up the river to St. Louis.

They'll wait there until Pa and me
catch the Rebs at Vicksburg.

*The waterfront at St. Louis, Missouri*

For two weeks Pa's been marching
his soldiers down here.
I could hear alligators
roaring in the swamps when
we marched through.
Now Pa's looking for a good place
to cross the river.
Tonight we're staying at a place
called Hard Times Plantation.
It's right on the river.
Thousands of Pa's soldiers
are camping here tonight.
Earlier this evening,
eight soldiers rowed across the river
in the dark.
They brought back a black fellow named Thomas.
He was a slave and he was glad to help Pa.
Pa talked to him in his tent.
Mr. Dana was there. So was I.
    "Now, Thomas," said Pa. "This is
what I want to do. I want to get my
army across the river, way below Vicksburg.

24

*Union soldiers in the swampy bayous*

Should I cross here, at Rodney?
Where would you cross, Thomas,
if you were me?"

"General, sir," said Thomas,
"you don't have to go down south
far as Rodney.
You can cross at Bruinsburg.
There's a good road there."

First Pa made sure that
Thomas was right.
Then Pa said, "We'll cross the
river tomorrow. At Bruinsburg!"

# 3. Missy and Queen

*April 30, 1863*

Pa gave me the slip today.
Pa and I and all the soldiers
crossed the river early this morning,
before the sun was up.
I fell asleep on the boat.
When I woke up, Pa and them were gone.
I hurried off that boat and
started walking after the army.
I haven't caught up with Pa yet!

*May 1, 1863*

I never found Pa yesterday.
This morning I could hear cannon
firing in the distance.

So I started down the road,
trying to catch up with the army.
Cannon and wagons and soldiers
kept going past me.
Mr. Dana was in one of the wagons.
He gave me a lift.
I was sure glad to see him.
Pretty soon we came to some cotton fields.
Then we saw a big plantation house.
There were lots of Negroes
at the gate.
The Negroes said this was Mrs. Prentiss' plantation.
Mr. Dana and I went up to the house.
Lots of our soldiers were in the yard.
Some were hitching horses and mules
to wagons and carriages.
Others were loading the wagons
with bags of cornmeal
and barrels of molasses, and hams,
and sweet potatoes and chickens.
There was a lady on the porch.
She was crying.

I guess it was Mrs. Prentiss.

"Can't somebody stop them!" she screamed.
"They're taking everything I own!"

MILLIKENS BEND

YAZOO RIV

VICKSB

GRANT'S ROUTE

MISSISSIPPI RIVER

HARD TIMES
LANDING

BRUINSBURG

PORT
GIBSON

## VICKSBURG CAMPAIGN

When Grant's soldiers marched from Milliken's Bend down through the swamps to
Hard Times Landing, and crossed the river at Bruinsburg, they were entering enemy
territory, and they were cutting themselves off from their supplies. No general since
Julius Caesar had dared to cut himself off as Grant did, but the

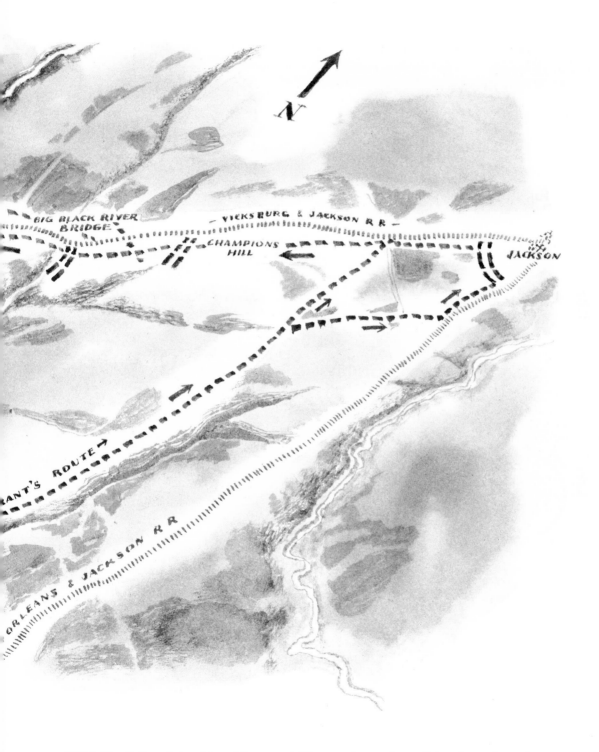

*N*

BIG BLACK RIVER
BRIDGE

VICKSBURG & JACKSON R R

CHAMPIONS
HILL

JACKSON

RANT'S ROUTE

ORLEANS & JACKSON R R

*"Old Man" found that his soldiers could live on the produce of the plantations along the way (like Mrs. Prentiss') and by May 19 Grant had burned the town of Jackson, defeated the Confederates at Champion's Hill and the Big Black River Bridge, and shut Pemberton up tight inside the siege lines at Vicksburg.*

She saw me and Mr. Dana.
"Is this the way you Yankees make war?"
she said. "Stealing from women!"

"General Grant needs food for his
soldiers," said Mr. Dana.
"And I'm afraid this boy and I
must take two of your horses, madam."

A little Negro boy heard Mr. Dana
and ran off to the stable.

He came back with two tired old horses.

"Toby! Don't you *dare* let them
have Missy and Queen!" said Mrs. Prentiss.

Mr. Dana and I jumped on the horses.
Missy and Queen sure were mighty old.
But we were glad to get them.

"I'm going 'long with the Yankee
soldiers myself, mistress," said Toby.
And he ran off down the road.

When the Union armies drew near, many slaves
ran away from their Southern masters and
joined the soldiers in blue. Later in the war,
the slaves were formed into regiments, to fight
for the Union, and for their freedom.

Mr. Dana was sorry to take
Mrs. Prentiss' horses,
but we had to find Pa in a hurry.

*Confederate and Union dead*

"This is a terrible war," said Mr. Dana.
"Yanks against Rebels. North against South.
We are all Americans.

I hope your father can put an end
to this war soon, Fred,
so that all the slaves can be free,
and we can all stop fighting."
Mr. Dana and I rode all day.
We found Pa before dark.
He had already won his first fight with
the Rebels, at a place called
Port Gibson.
He laughed when he saw Mr. Dana and me
shambling along on Missy and Queen.

# 4. The Veteran

*May 14, 1863*

Mr. Dana and I have stuck with Pa
and the rest of the soldiers
ever since we caught up with them.
I've seen a lot of fighting.
I've been in two battles.
Every night I sit with Pa
in his tent.
Pa's always reading maps,
and sending telegrams to
Washington, D.C.
Mr. Dana says one time, some people
wanted to change Pa for another general.
But Mr. Lincoln said, "I can't

spare the man. He fights."
Mr. Lincoln is the President
of the United States.
Mr. Lincoln's right about Pa.
Pa's sure making these Rebs run.
But Pa says Mr. Lincoln doesn't think Pa knows
how to take Vicksburg.
Today, Pa and I were in Jackson.
The Reb soldiers ran when we got there.
Pa said we must tear up the railroad
and burn the factories and the
cotton bales.
So the soldiers tore up the railroad.
And they burned the factories and
all the cotton.
Then we rode away, toward Vicksburg.


*May 17, 1863*

The biggest battle so far
was yesterday, at Champion's Hill.
Pa won again.

*President Abraham Lincoln*

*Union armies wrecked locomotives and railroad tracks in much of the South*

Mr. Dana says Pa is the
most determined man he ever saw.
This morning we chased the Rebs
to the Big Black River.
The Rebs were fighting to keep us from
crossing. Every time the cannon boomed,
the moss on the oak trees shook.
I got sort of wounded in the leg.
Pretty soon the Rebs had to run.
They burned the railroad trestle.
Then the whole shooting match skedaddled.
Tomorrow we'll chase them some more.

*May 19, 1863*

Today Pa shut the Rebs up
inside Vicksburg. They're surrounded.
General Pemberton has nowhere to go.
Pemberton is the Rebs' general.
Pa says the Rebs have to
stay there and starve

*Gen. John C. Pemberton, C.S.A.*

until they give up.
Pa says there's no telling
how long they can hold out.

*Rebel soldier*

*Yankee soldier*

Then Pa said, "How's the leg, veteran?"

"It's just a scratch," I said.
"How come you call me 'veteran'?"

"Well, Fred," Pa said, "Cump Sherman
and Mr. Dana and all the men
are calling you the veteran,
now that you been wounded."

I didn't let on,
but the soldiers have a name
for Pa too. They call him
"The Old Man."

# 5. A Birthday Present for Nellie

*May 30, 1863*

Vicksburg is still holding out.
Cannon boom night and day.
We hear that some of the folks in the city
are digging caves.
They're hiding in them, to try
to get away from Pa's cannon fire.
In some places, our trenches
are real near the Rebel trenches.
The soldiers can talk back and forth.
Our men have plenty of bread and coffee.
The Rebs have plenty of tobacco.
Sometimes they swap.

Pa hopes this war will end soon.
It's my birthday today.
I sure have plenty to tell Ma

and Nellie and Buck and Jesse,
when I get home.
They sent me some stuff for my birthday.

*A Union battery outside the siege lines at Vicksburg*

Nellie's got a birthday coming, too.
She'll be eight on the Fourth of July.

Vicksburg is still holding out.
Pa says he's got 220 cannon
shooting at Pemberton.
Pemberton's brave, but he
can't beat Pa!
Mr. Dana says they're running out of
food in Vicksburg.
He says they have nothing to eat
but mules and rats.
Pa told me something funny
about Mr. Dana tonight.
It's something Mr. Dana thinks
Pa doesn't know.
Pa says Mr. Lincoln sent Mr. Dana
down here to keep an eye on Pa!
Pa doesn't care.

*Inside the lines at Vicksburg*

Pa says folks used to tell
President Lincoln,
"General Grant drinks too much whiskey."
Pa says Mr. Lincoln said,

"I just wish I knew what brand
he uses. I'd send a barrel
to all my *other* generals."


*July 3, 1863*

Vicksburg is still holding out.
Pa says the Rebs can't fight much longer.
Mr. Dana says they're printing
their newspaper on old rolls of wallpaper.
He says they don't have many
mules and rats left to eat.
The Rebs put out white flags today.
Pa's over there right now
with General Pemberton.
They're under that oak tree.
Mr. Dana says Pemberton
will have to surrender.


*July 4, 1863*

The Rebs surrendered today!
At ten this morning,

*Brave Confederate soldiers, like these, held out for forty-seven days in the besieged town, until Pemberton had to surrender Vicksburg to Grant.*

the Rebels marched out and
put down their rifles.
And at eleven o'clock, Pa and
all his soldiers marched into Vicksburg.
We all went to the courthouse.
Cump Sherman and Mr. Dana were there.
The band played "The Star-Spangled Banner."
We watched while they ran the flag
right up to the top of the pole.
Then Pa sent a telegram to
Mr. Lincoln, and another one to
Ma and them, in St. Louis.
This time Mr. Lincoln sent
a telegram right back to Pa!
   It said: "Dear General Grant,
You were right, and I was wrong.
Signed, A. Lincoln."
Mr. Lincoln meant that Pa had been
right and everybody else wrong
about how to capture Vicksburg.

*Grant's troops march into Vicksburg, July 4, 1863.*

"Pa," I said, "guess what?
Today is Nellie's birthday!"
"That's right!" said Pa.
"It's the Fourth of July."
"Vicksburg sure is a first-rate
birthday present for Nellie," I said.
Cump Sherman and Mr. Dana and Pa laughed.
"Vicksburg," said Mr. Dana,
"is a first-rate present
for the whole country."

## ABOUT THIS STORY

In 1863, when this story takes place, the United States was fighting the Civil War. And for the first and only time in our history, there were two presidents in our country at the same time. For during the war years (1861–1865) Abraham Lincoln, in Washington, D.C., was the leader of the Northern states; and Jefferson Davis, in Richmond, Virginia, was the leader of the Southern, or Confederate, states. For four terrible years the North and South fought—Yankees against Rebels—until the North finally won.

Most of the incidents in this story actually happened. Frederick Dent Grant, oldest son of General Ulysses S. Grant, was twelve years old when he and his father set out to capture Vicksburg. By the time the city fell (on July 4, 1863, the very same day that the battle of Gettysburg was being fought in Pennsylvania) Fred had turned thirteen. He did not keep a diary of what he saw, but he remembered it all for the rest of his life.

When Pemberton surrendered, more than 30,000 Confederate soldiers were captured. The Vicksburg fight was one of the most important campaigns in the Civil War. Grant's victory cut the Confederacy in two, and gave the North full control of the Mississippi River, so that, as President Lincoln said, "the Father of Waters again goes unvexed to the sea."

Most important of all, the victory at Vicksburg showed the country that the North really had a good chance of winning the Civil War. And it showed President Lincoln (and Charles A. Dana, his observer from the War Department) that his best general was U. S. Grant.

Lincoln later asked Grant to come to the White House, where, on March 9, 1864, he put him in charge of all the soldiers in blue. Fred was there, too!

In later years, Mr. Dana became editor of a famous newspaper, the New York *Sun*. Fred Grant went to West Point and served as a brigadier general in the Spanish-American War and later in the Philippines. General William Tecumseh ("Cump") Sherman helped his friend Grant defeat the armies of the Confederacy. At the end of the Civil War, General Ulysses S. Grant accepted General Robert E. Lee's surrender at Appomattox and later became the eighteenth president of the United States, serving from 1869 to 1877.

One word more about the Grant family: it must have been an unusually happy one. Each of the four children was convinced that he was his father's favorite—Fred, because he was the oldest; Buck (U. S. Grant, Jr.), because he was named for his father; Nellie, because she was the only girl; and Jesse, because he was the youngest!